This book belongs to:

_ _ _ _ _ _ _ _ _ _ _ _ _

_ _ _ _ _ _ _ _ _ _ _ _ _

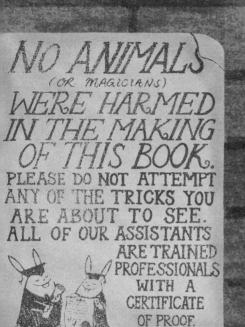

BEADLE, JONES, EVETT & HACKFORT & TEARLE

for
**JONNY,
ISLA &
JACKSON**

FIRST PUBLISHED IN GREAT BRITAIN
IN 2016 BY ANDERSEN PRESS LTD.,
THIS PAPERBACK EDITION FIRST PUBLISHED
IN 2017 BY ANDERSEN PRESS LTD.

20 VAUXHALL BRIDGE ROAD, LONDON SW1V 2SA

COPYRIGHT © MEG McLAREN 2016

THE RIGHT OF MEG McLAREN TO BE IDENTIFIED
AS THE AUTHOR AND ILLUSTRATOR OF THIS WORK
HAS BEEN ASSERTED BY HER IN ACCORDANCE WITH THE
COPYRIGHT, DESIGNS AND PATENTS ACT. 1988

ALL RIGHTS RESERVED

10 9 8 7 6 5 4 3 2 1

Rebecca Garrill
ART DIRECTION

PRINTED &
BOUND IN
CHINA

Edited by
Libby Hamilton

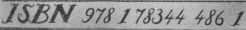

BRITISH LIBRARY CATALOGUING IN PUBLICATION DATA AVAILABLE

ISBN 978 1 78344 486 1

MEG McLAREN

MONSIEUR LAPIN PRESENTS

LIFE
IS
MAGIC

AN~ANDERSEN~PRESS~PRODUCTION

The hardest part of any magic show is picking the right assistant.

Not everyone is a born performer.

Some suffer from stage fright,

while others have a terrible sense of timing.

And not everyone understands props.

But Houdini the rabbit was a natural.

TADAA!

He **loved** magic.

And he had a knack for bringing the team together.

From the after-show treats,

to the pre-show
checks,

EUCH!

Houdini took care of everyone and everything.

So one night,
when things
went wrong...

Houdini carried on with the show.

The crowd thought it was the best trick **ever**.

But the magician wasn't too pleased...

when they discovered his new role might be permanent.

As rehearsals got underway, not everyone was impressed by Houdini's talent.

NOM...

And their new boss seemed
far too busy.

But word soon spread.

Houdini's hard work began to pay off
as people flocked to see the show.

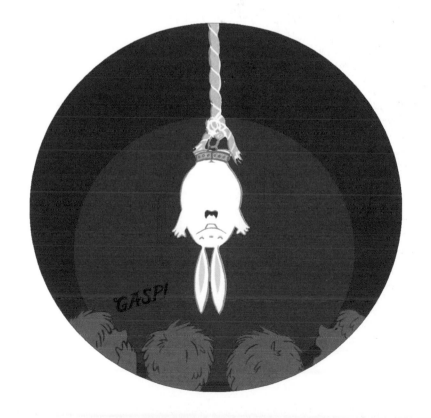

The more daring
his tricks became,
the more the crowd
loved him.

Houdini was a hit.

Night after night the audience cheered.

CLAP CLAP CLAP CLAP CLAP CLAP CLAP CLAP CLAP Clap clap Clap CLAP CLAP CLAP CLAP CLAP CLAP

But for Houdini, the
excitement was fading.

Though he'd enjoyed his time in the spotlight,

someone else needed it more.

So he gathered
the team together.
On the last night of his
sell-out tour, Houdini
would attempt...

Which goes to show

that sometimes rabbits
(and people)

do the most unexpected things...

because life is **truly** magical when you share it.

SOLD OUT

FEATURING
HOUDINI
AND THE
HOPPERS

STAGE
DOOR

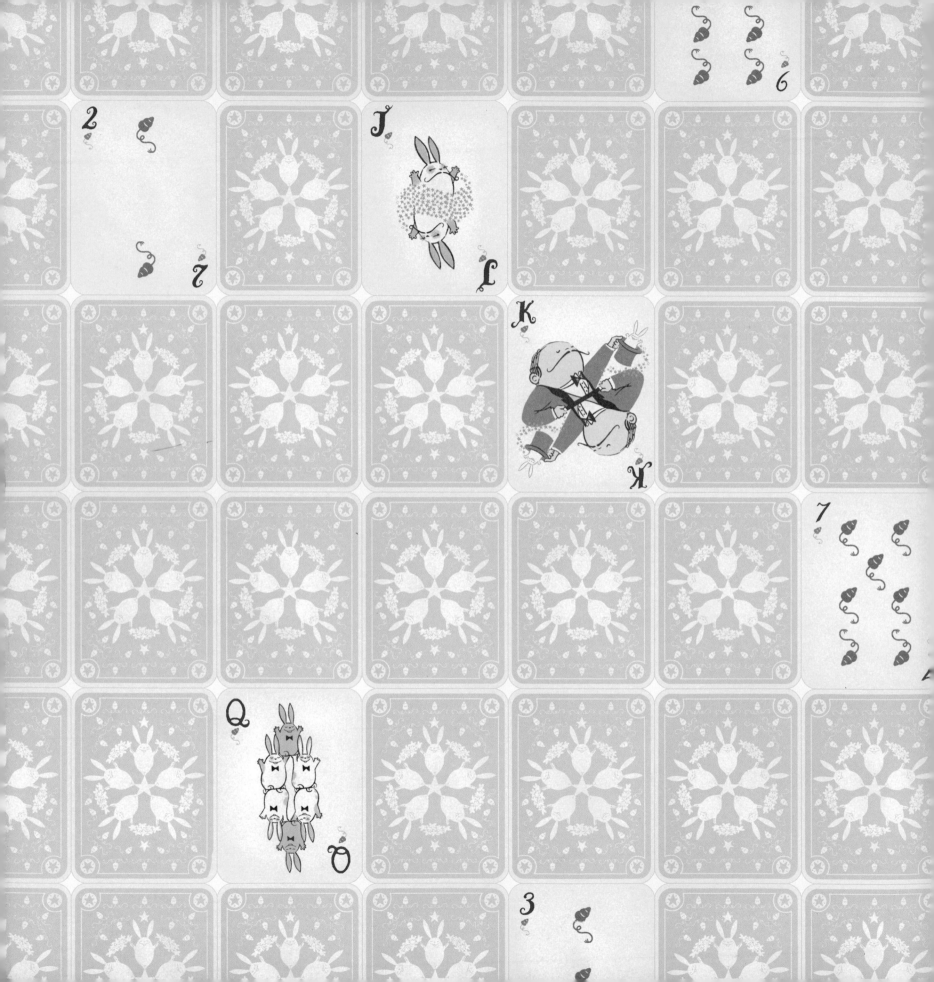